SNOWBOARD
STRUGGLE

BY JAKE MADDOX

text by
Brandon Terrell

a capstone imprint

Jake Maddox JV books are published by
Stone Arch Books
A Capstone imprint
1710 Roe Crest Drive
North Mankato, Minnesota 56003
www.mycapstone.com

Library of Congress Cataloging-in-Publication Data is available on the
Library of Congress website

ISBN: 978-1-4965-3980-9 (hardcover) 978-1-4965-3984-7 (paperback)
978-1-4965-3988-5 (ebook PDF)

Summary: Alex loves to ski and hang out with his best friend, Kevin. But when a new kid with a mysterious home life and some killer moves on the slopes joins the ski team, Alex must find out who he wants to side with and what kind of person he wants to be.

Art Director: Nathan Gassman
Designer: Sarah Bennett
Production Specialist: Katy LaVigne

Photo Credits:
Shutterstock: Aaron Amat, design element, Brocreative, design element, DeanHarty, design element, Dmitry Kalinovsky, design element, hin255, design element, irin-k, design element, Ivan Smuk, cover, Volt Collection, design element

Printed and bound in the United States of America.
009622F16

TABLE OF CONTENTS

CHAPTER 1

FIELD TRIP

Thirteen-year-old Alex Landry scraped frost from the cold school bus window, pressed his nose so close his breath fogged up the glass again, and peered out. Filling the horizon outside were the towering ski slopes of Mount Kingsford.

"Black diamond trails, here we come!" a voice behind Alex called out. Kevin Frye, Alex's best friend since the day they first shared crayons and a Ninja Mummy coloring book in kindergarten, leaned over the back of Alex's seat.

A throat cleared loudly from the front of the bus. "Mr. Frye," one of the chaperones, their biology teacher, Mr. Carlson, said. "Please be seated."

Kevin dropped back into his seat with a whump.

Alex, Kevin, and the rest of the eighth graders from Kingsford Middle School were going to spend the day skiing and snowboarding on a field trip. For some, it would be the only time that winter they'd hit the snowy Wisconsin slopes. For Alex and his friends, though, it was the start of a winter filled with downhill fun.

Alex had been a regular at Mount Kingsford for years. The collection of ski passes dangling from his coat proved it. He'd been snowboarding for as long as he could remember; he loved it more than anything else in the world. He and Kevin were members of the Kingsford Snowboard Cross — or SBX — team. So were their friends Eddie Dean, a massive middle schooler who looked like a figure from Norse mythology on a snowboard, and Tia

Lin, a spark plug of energy. The first team practice was days away, and their trip today was a good chance to shake off a summer's worth of rust from their snowboarding skills.

The bus rumbled into the parking lot. A second bus filled with Kingsford students pulled in behind it. Kids in bulky snowsuits filled the aisle. They swished against one another, their boots clunking on the muddy floor.

"Let's go!" Kevin pushed into the aisle.

"Dude, chill," Tia said with a laugh. She should really have taken her own advice, though, because she elbowed in front of Kevin.

Though the sun was blinding, it was bitterly cold. Alex's boots crunched and squeaked in the snow. He jammed his hat over his ears and breathed deep.

He loved the way the air numbed his fingers and cheeks, loved how each inhalation turned his lungs to ice and froze the inside of his nose.

It's a great day to snowboard, Alex thought with a smile.

The two busloads of students headed to the chalet, a three-story stone and wood building. They flocked toward the rental counter. Alex and his friends, however, went to the chalet's locker rooms, where large metal lockers held their boards and gear. They paid a steep rental fee for the lockers — according to Alex's parents — but not having to lug around a snowboard each time they came was worth it.

No one talked about which run they were going to hit first; they already knew. They always knew. Their destination was Ridgeline, a blue intermediate trail in the back of the mountain, flanked on either side by trees.

They hit the ski lift and made their way up the slopes for the first time.

Alex rode in the two-person chair alongside Eddie. He felt like he'd lost a bet. Eddie took up most of the chair, leaving Alex a sliver of space. As they rode up the mountain, Alex's eyes drifted from Kevin and Tia in the chair in front of them to the trail below, a black diamond named Jagged Boulder.

A streak of color carved down the trail. A snowboarder in a bright yellow coat sailed off a berm and landed softly in the heart of the course. Alex couldn't get a close look at the person, though; they were there one second, gone the next.

When they made it to Ridgeline, the quartet stood shoulder to shoulder at the start of the run.

"Let's do this," Alex said, sliding on his goggles.

Kevin offered up a gloved fist, and Alex bumped it.

They tilted their boards and made their descent.

The first time down a run was like the tumblers of a lock clicking into place. No matter how long it had been since his last ride down the powder, Alex knew how his body would respond to the board, to the hills and their unique obstacles.

He crouched low and leaned into each turn. One gloved hand danced along the edge of the snow. Trees zipped past in his periphery. He hit a berm and caught air, twisting his board up and rotating in a 180. He landed riding fakie, with his opposite foot forward, until he hit the next bump and switched back.

Kevin kept pace at first, as he always did. Before long, though, he pulled ahead of Alex. Kevin was the best boarder on the SBX team, and everyone knew it. Especially Kevin. Eddie lumbered behind them, with Tia carving circles around him.

At the end of the run, Alex twisted his board and pressed his heels down. He came to a skittering stop next to Kevin. The others joined them seconds later.

"That felt good," Alex said, lifting off his goggles.

"Ready for more?" Kevin asked impatiently.

"I'm just getting started," Alex said.

He unlatched one foot from its binding and pushed off across the hard-packed snow. As he reached the lift, Alex caught a flicker of yellow again. He looked left, where the base of Jagged Boulder spilled out.

The person he'd seen earlier — the streak of yellow that, as it turned out, looked to be a boy about his own age — raced down the slope. As Alex watched, the kid hit a jump and grabbed the back of the deck, twisting in a backside indy. He landed without a hitch and kept rocketing down the slope.

Dang, Alex thought, *Jagged Boulder is the toughest trail out here, and he makes it look easy.* He remembered the last time he'd taken Boulder, how he'd wound up with bruises on both arms after coming off one of the trail's small, cliff-like jumps from trying a 180 in midair.

"Come on," Kevin said, unaware of the skilled boarder who had Alex transfixed. He shoved Alex. "Load up."

Alex slid forward and waited for the lift to whisk him back to the top of the slopes.

They made several more runs before breaking for lunch, and a handful more after they ate. As the end of the school day neared, the buses arrived back in the lot.

Alex and his friends returned their gear to their lockers and walked to the bus. While Kevin bragged about his sweet skills to Eddie and Tia, Alex spied the kid in the yellow coat walking alone, hands shoved into his pockets. His coat was ripped under one arm, a puff of dirty white fleece sticking out and making him look like a torn teddy bear in need of stitching.

"Scuse me," the kid muttered as he breezed past Alex and Kevin and boarded one of the buses.

I gotta figure out who that dude is, Alex thought. *Because he makes everyone else on our SBX team look like they belong on the bunny hill.*

CHAPTER 2

THE NEW KID

The next time Alex saw the boy in the yellow coat, it was in the cafeteria the following day during lunch period. Kingsford Middle School wasn't that large, but it was big enough to not know every face that walked the halls at every given moment.

Alex walked through the cafeteria, plastic tray filled with pizza rolls, chicken nuggets, and tater tots. One section of the tray was devoted to a puddle of ketchup.

The boy sat alone, tucked in a cafeteria corner. He had close-cropped dark hair, and even though he was seated, Alex could tell he was tall and skinny. He looked bored, picking apart a sandwich from a brown bag lunch. A battered backpack rested on the table beside him; he had one arm slumped over it.

As Alex walked closer, he noticed a skateboard leaning against the seat next to the kid. A pass for Skate Kings, the skate park over in the Kingsford warehouse district, was hooked to his backpack.

He was intriguing, this snowboarder who made black diamond trails look like backyard hills.

"Alex! Over here!" Kevin's voice cut through the loud cafeteria. Alex saw his friend waving. He, Eddie, and Tia sat at their usual table.

Alex lowered his head and beelined through the cafeteria. He cast a glance back and saw the boy rolling a slice of ham from his sandwich and popping it into his mouth.

"What's the deal?" Kevin asked as Alex dropped his tray with a clatter to the table and slid in next to Tia. She was drawing intricate tattoos in blue ink on her forearm. "You forget where we sit every day?"

"Yeah," Eddie added, "You getting Old Timer's disease or something?"

"It's Alzheimer's, Eddie," Alex said, laughing.

"Sorry, I forgot," Eddie joked.

"Anybody know what's up with the new kid?" Alex asked. He glanced back; the kid was still dissecting his sandwich.

"What do you mean?" Kevin asked.

Tia shrugged. "He was in my Civics class this morning. Don't know his name."

Alex thought back to the kid defying gravity and whipping around in midair on his board. On a black diamond trail, to boot. "I saw him on Jagged Boulder yesterday," he explained. "Maybe I should recruit him for SBX."

"He's that good?" Eddie asked.

"He's better than good," Alex said.

"First boardercross practice is after school tomorrow," Tia said. "Coach Gregg is always looking for new recruits."

"If his skills are solid," Eddie added, "he should show up."

Kevin took another bite of food and smiled. "You want to recruit him?" he asked Alex. "Man, you could fill a solar system with the number of things you never follow through on. I give it one day before you decide to give up." He laughed, and the others joined in.

Alex felt his ears burn at the dig from Kevin. "All I'm saying is, dude needs to be on the team," he said.

He decided right then and there that he was going to make sure of it. No matter what it took.

CHAPTER 3

SKATE KINGS

When the final school bell rang, Alex scanned the halls for the kid's bright yellow jacket. He didn't see him anywhere.

But he might have an idea where to find him.

Eddie was sitting at the top of the stone steps just outside the school's front door. "We're heading to Kevin's to rip it up," he said as he mimed playing a video game controller. "He's got *Zom-Borg 7*. You in?"

Alex nodded. "Yeah," he said. "I have to make a stop first, though."

"Whatever." Eddie stood. "Probably going to grab burritos on the way. I'll get you something."

"Cool." Alex shouldered his backpack and started walking.

It was a little warmer than the day before. The sun was masked by gray clouds. Alex's "stop" was a bit of a hike, so he bundled himself up and began to hurry down the sidewalk.

As Alex walked, he thought about his conversation at lunch. Sure, Kevin had been joking when he said Alex didn't follow through on things. But his words rung true, whether he meant them or not. They made Alex think about all the times he was too nervous or scared to commit to something.

Not anymore, he thought.

By the time he reached Skate Kings, Alex's eyes were watering, and his cheeks were frozen. The building was identical to all the other warehouses on the block: corrugated metal, large delivery doors. The only hint that Skate Kings was there at all was a small red door at the top of a set of cement steps. A sign above it featured a crown made from a skateboard.

Music pulsed inside the skate park. The hollow, metal walls made it echo and distort. The park wasn't much; it had a half-pipe in the center, and a section to the side with rails and stainless steel ramps.

It wasn't crowded and Alex lucked out right away. The new kid was skating in the half-pipe and getting massive air. He whipped his body around in tight 360s, as though he could control gravity. Alex perched himself on a plastic chair, watching until the boarder came down for a breather.

The kid grabbed a candy bar from a vending machine, pulled out a chair at a table near Alex with a screech of legs on concrete, and dropped into it. Alex was nervous about approaching him.

Suck it up, man, he told himself. *You can do this.*

With slow, timid steps, he walked over.

"Hey," Alex said.

The kid turned and stared at him with a mouth full of chocolate and nougat.

"You're new at Kingsford Middle," Alex said, stating the obvious. "I . . . I saw you on the half-pipe." He shifted on his feet. *Man, I sound like a dork.* "Pretty sick moves. I'm more of a snowboarder."

"Yeah," the kid said. "I recognize you from the slopes. And the cafeteria."

"Yeah." Alex adjusted his backpack. "Uh, I saw you, too. At Mount Kingsford. You're pretty good on a snowboard."

"Thanks." The kid chomped another bite of candy bar.

"Ever think about joining the school team?" Alex asked.

The kid chewed, then asked, "There's a school snowboard team?"

"Well, yeah," Alex said.

The kid chuckled and held up his battered skateboard. "I've had this deck since I was a noob. Changed the grip tape I don't know how many times. But grip tape is cheap. I can't afford to buy snowboarding gear. The stuff you get at the rental shop is good for blowing off steam on the hill, but you can't race with it."

"Well, if that's your reason, I've got you covered," Alex said. "I have some old stuff you can borrow. We can go to my place and get it right now, if you want."

The kid was quiet. He stared off toward the half-pipe, watching a young skater tentatively roll from one side to the other.

Finally, when Alex couldn't take the awkward silence anymore, he said, "Whatever. Just thought I'd throw it out there."

As Alex began to walk away, though, the kid asked, "Why would you do that?"

Alex turned back. "Do what?"

"Loan me your gear. I don't even know your name."

Alex shrugged. "I just want to help my team."

Another screech came from the chair as the kid stood up. "Yeah, all right," he said. "I'll take you up on it."

"Cool." Alex held out a hand. "Alex Landry."

The kid shook it. "Miles Vaughn."

Together, the two boys slipped back into the bitter winter evening. Miles dropped his deck to the sidewalk and lazily pushed off. Alex shuffled along beside him as they began the cold trek toward the Landry home.

CHAPTER 4

DINNER IS SERVED

"Dang, dude," Miles said with a low whistle. "Living the high life."

The two boys walked through Alex's neighborhood. Miles had ditched riding his deck; it was tucked under one arm. Instead, he balanced on the curb, taking in his surroundings.

Alex had lived his whole life in the part of Kingsford known as Old K. The houses in Old K were enormous, with lawns outlined by trees and high fences. Alex had never given it a second thought. But Miles's comment made him suddenly very aware of how ridiculously large the homes were. It made him weirdly uncomfortable.

They cut down Elm Street, just a few houses away from Kevin's. Alex could see bikes lying in the snowbank off the driveway, under a pool of light from a street lamp.

Oh, crap, Alex thought. *I totally forgot about Zom-Borg 7 and burritos.*

For a second he felt a pang of guilt but then shrugged. *Oh, well.* They'd be just fine without him.

The Landry house was a two-story Tudor with white siding and red brick. Dead ivy flaked with ice crystals snaked up the walls.

"What do your parents do for a living?" Miles asked as Alex punched in the code for the garage and one of the three doors rattled open.

"Mom's a lawyer," Alex answered. "Dad works with computers. Beats me exactly what he does with them, though."

No one was home yet. They entered the dark house, flicking on lights as they went. Alex led Miles to the basement storage room and switched on the light. Walls of shelves were filled with bins of Christmas and Halloween decorations, baby toys, and clothes.

"Man, you have a lot of stuff," Miles said, plucking a plastic candy cane from a shelf and wielding it like a sword.

"Yeah," Alex said. "I guess so." That feeling of embarrassment came wriggling back. He tried to shrug it away by directing his energy at a stack of boxes in one corner. Behind them, leaning against the wall, were some old snowboards and boots. "Here they are."

He dug out a board and held it out to Miles. It was blue with the white outline of a dragon wrapped around it.

Miles took the board from Alex and inspected it. "Cool. Thanks, man."

"Sure thing," Alex said. "You totally have to join the team, Miles. You're good."

Alex snagged a pair of boots to go with the board, and the two boys made their way back to the kitchen. As they did, the door to the garage suddenly swung open, and Alex's mom came whisking in, arms full. A colorful stocking cap sat atop her head.

"Alex!" she said. "Give me a hand, would you?"

The sweet aroma of egg rolls and kung pao chicken wafted from the plastic bags in her hands. Alex's stomach rumbled like a slumbering animal waking up. He grabbed the bags and set them on the counter.

"Who's your friend?" his mom chirped.

"Miles Vaughn," Alex said. "He's new."

Miles set the snowboard and boots down like he'd been caught trying to steal them.

"Well, good thing you're here, Miles," Alex's mom said. "Because I bought way too much food."

She hung her coat on a hook near the door, then grabbed plates from a cupboard.

"Oh, I . . . can't stay," Miles said.

"Too late." Alex's mom added silverware to the stack of plates and began to set the table. "Do you need to call your parents?"

"No, ma'am," Miles said quietly.

The garage door opened again, and Alex's dad entered, followed by his little brother, Beckett. Beckett's nose was buried in a handheld game console, his face nearly hidden by his mop of brown curls. The game squawked as Alex's dad said, "Sorry we're late."

"You're right on time," his mom said. "Alex brought a friend for dinner. Miles."

"Hello, sir."

"Miles, welcome." Alex's dad put a hand on Beckett's shoulder and directed him toward the dining room. "Time to shut it down, kiddo," he said.

Alex and his family had a rule: no electronics at the dinner table. His mom had set up a ceramic bowl on a wooden hutch. As he walked to the table, Alex dug out his cell phone and dropped it into the bowl.

He nodded at Miles. "Resistance is futile."

"I'm good," Miles said, looking away. Alex shrugged and didn't push it.

The two boys took a seat next to one another as Beckett dumped his console alongside Alex's phone.

Dinner was a whirlwind. Neither of Alex's parents were good cooks; his dad joked that the "best cookbook ever written was a take-out menu." They filled their plates with rice and chicken and veggies from the white paper containers.

"So, Miles," Alex's mom said. "Your family just moved here?"

"Yes, ma'am," Miles said. "From Milwaukee." He shifted on his feet.

Alex realized that he'd been so concerned with Miles's snowboarding abilities that he hadn't even asked about his family.

"What do your parents do?" Alex's dad asked.

"It's . . . just my mom," Miles said. "She works a lot. My aunt comes over most nights, too, though. Like tonight."

"Do you have siblings?"

Alex was beginning to think his parents' barrage of questions was an interrogation. Miles looked like he felt the same way.

"Yeah," he answered. "Two brothers and a sister."

Alex caught his dad opening his mouth for another question and interrupted him. "Miles is going to join the boardercross team. He's really good," he blurted out.

"Oh, that's wonderful," Alex's mom said.

"You'll have fun," his dad added. "Bunch of good kids on that team." He took a bite of food before adding, "That is, when they're not eating every crumb of food in my pantry."

When they'd finished their meal, Alex helped clear the table before showing Miles to the door. "Thanks for dinner," Miles said to Alex's parents.

"You're welcome — anytime," Alex's mom said. "Do you need a ride home?" The expression on Miles's face was thankful but shocked, like that was the last thing he'd expected.

"Nah, I'm good. It won't take long," he said, looking down. "I'll get home before dark."

"Dude, we'll give you a ride home," Alex said, looking out the window at the sun just starting to set. "You have things to carry."

But Miles shook his head adamantly. "No. I'll get home myself."

Alex shrugged and passed off the snowboard and boots as Miles gathered up his things. He shared a look with his mother, but she raised her eyebrows like, "It's his call."

"Thanks again, man," Miles said.

"No prob."

Alex stood in the door frame as Miles walked down the drive, snowboard slung over one shoulder, boots and deck cradled in the other. He gave one last wave as he reached the street.

"See you on the slopes!" Alex called out.

CHAPTER 5

NO-SHOW

He didn't, though.

In fact, Alex didn't see Miles Vaughn at all the following day.

He looked for him during class, at lunch. He wasn't there. After school, when Alex told their coach about the new kid who was bound to dazzle the team, he anticipated Miles bursting into the locker room. He didn't. When the bus to Mount Kingsford left with the boys and girls of the SBX team, Alex crossed his fingers that Miles would come running up. Nothing. Even after arriving at the slopes, Alex hoped for Miles to be there, snowboard in hand, smugly saying, "What took you so long?"

But there was no grand entrance.

"What's the deal?" Kevin asked as Alex glanced over the group milling around the chalet. "You looking for someone?"

"I guess not," Alex said, defeated.

"Listen up!" Coach Gregg called out. He was in his late twenties with dreadlocked hair hidden beneath a wool stocking cap. The school wanted the team to call him Mr. Paulsen, or Coach Paulsen, but nobody did. He was Coach Gregg, and he cringed if you called him anything else. "First day back, so nothing fancy. Take some runs, loosen up. We'll work on gates in an hour. Got it?"

Alex and the others nodded.

Kevin beelined for the chair lift. Alex followed. "Want to make a run down Jagged Boulder?" Kevin asked.

Jagged Boulder was the black diamond trail Alex saw Miles navigating during the field trip.

"Coach said to take it easy," Alex said.

Kevin gave him a playful shove. "Come on," he said. "If that dork in the yellow coat can rock this course, so can we."

"All right." Alex waited beside Kevin as the next chair swung toward them. He almost added, *That dork's name is Miles and, p.s., he's not a dork*, but the idea drifted away as the lift chair jerked against his knees. He sat quickly, and they were whisked into the sky.

They rode up in silence, feet dangling in thin air, boards clacking together with each sway of the lift. Alex looked down at the curving lines cut into the powder by passing skiers and boarders, like a freeway map traced in the snow.

Kevin didn't stop after the lift dropped them at the top of the mountain. He headed directly for Jagged Boulder. Alex tailed him, his mind drifting to the field trip, to Miles and his yellow coat sailing down Boulder like it was a backyard hill.

I can't believe he didn't show up today, Alex thought as he took a deep breath, slipped on his goggles, and followed Kevin down the difficult trail.

The two friends navigated the tight curves and jumps. Kevin was in his usual spot in front of Alex. Alex didn't know Jagged Boulder as well as the other trails. On a normal day, his instincts would take over to guide him down.

But he couldn't stop thinking about Miles being a no-show. The dude had talent, and he'd promised he'd be at practice with Alex's gear.

The one time I follow through on something, and it's a huge bust. What happened?

"Head's up!" Kevin's voice cut through the fog. Alex's daydreaming had caused him to drift. He saw the evergreen approaching fast and cut back, narrowly missing it.

That was close.

Alex cursed himself for losing focus. He couldn't believe that he'd been so preoccupied that he'd taken his attention off the course — especially on such a treacherous trail. It was a dangerous move, and he was fortunate he hadn't biffed hard on the first run of the day.

* * *

King's Crown, one of the slopes' back trails, was set up as a boardercross course. It wasn't terribly steep, but there were gates at the top, a rhythm section of berms, followed by S-shaped curves dotted with colored flags. During the summer, Alex and his friends spent time practicing at an indoor simulation of gates inside the chalet. But those were nothing compared to the real deal, to staring down at the course below and feeling the wind bite at exposed skin.

Coach Gregg had them work on getting out of the starting gates quickly. "Reaction time is everything," he said. "Know the cadence, be ready for it. First group, you're up."

Alex slid into position. Kevin rode next to him. Handles were set up on either side of the gate, along with a foot-high strip of metal. Alex tapped the nose of his board against the metal for luck.

"Riders, ready!" Coach Gregg shouted.

Alex slid back, stretched his arms out, still holding the handles. He looked down at the snowy course.

"Attention!"

The gate could drop at any moment during the next five seconds. Alex had to be focused.

"Go!"

The metal strip slammed down. Alex pulled himself forward with all his might. He shot out of the gate alongside four other racers. The wind cut through his helmet, across his cheeks.

"Good!" He could barely hear Coach Gregg shout at them as they maneuvered the rolling hills.

His board bucked and swerved under his feet. Beside him, Kevin raced down the hill full-tilt.

Since they weren't practicing full runs yet, Alex's group eased up, taking the turns lazily. Most of them did, anyway. Kevin roared down the course like he was in the middle of a race. When Alex reached the bottom of the hill, he slid up to the lift. Kevin was waiting for him.

"Slowpoke," he said.

"You know we're not racing yet, right?" Alex said.

Kevin shrugged. "Backing down is for losers," he said. "I never give up on anything."

They practiced gates until the sun was swallowed by the mountain and the sky was left ablaze in orange and pink light.

"Bus'll be here any minute," Coach Gregg informed the team after they'd stored their gear and gathered near the chalet. "Hang tight. Great practice today, team."

Eddie leaned against the rack, which protested against his weight. Kevin complained that he wanted one last run before they left. Tia's hair stuck to her face, even after being freed from her helmet. "Anybody else's arms feel like JELL-O?" she asked.

"I'd raise my hand," Eddie said, "but I don't have the strength."

Alex said nothing. Instead, he stared at the base of Jagged Boulder, and recalled the first time he saw Miles carving down the trail. How impressive he'd looked, how his moves rivaled those of even Kevin.

Alex needed to find Miles and ask him why he'd flaked out on practice.

CHAPTER 6

MILES IN REAL LIFE

Alex had a good idea of where to find Miles. Sure enough, as he walked into Skate Kings, he spied him sitting in a booth, sweatshirt hood covering his head, scribbling in a notebook. A pair of earbuds snaked from his hood.

Miles didn't seem surprised to see Alex.

"Hey," Miles said. He pulled down his hood and yanked on his headphone cord. Both earbuds popped out in unison.

"Where were you?" Alex asked. "You missed practice."

Miles shrugged. "I decided not to go." He gathered up his things and shoved them into his backpack.

"What?"

"Sorry, man," Miles said. "It's not my crowd."

Alex was confused. "What do you mean, 'not my crowd'? I told Coach Gregg you'd be there. I stuck my neck out for you."

Miles shrugged. "I'll bring your board back to you."

Alex didn't know Miles very well, but he knew when someone wasn't telling him the whole story. This was one of those times. "What's really going on?" he asked.

Miles eyed him, like he was judging whether or not to trust Alex. Finally, he stood and grabbed his skateboard. "You want the whole story?" he said. "Then follow me."

Alex didn't question him; he followed Miles out of the skate park and back into the cold evening.

Miles dropped his deck to the sidewalk, climbed aboard, and pushed off. Alex hurried along in his wake.

Miles wove his deck around slick spots on the sidewalk and chunks of ice and snow in the road. Alex could see why the kid was a talented snowboarder. Some of the skills needed to ride a skateboard translated well to the slopes. Balance. Instincts. Awareness.

Miles had all three.

They reached a neighborhood Alex had hardly been to before. He knew a couple of places in the area — his dad's favorite hole-in-the-wall pizzeria was down a few blocks, and he could see Kingsford Junkyard in the distance — but he didn't know anyone who lived here. The houses were one-story ramblers, not much to look at and not kept in very good shape.

They reached a tan house with dirty white trim and shutters. Spindly brown evergreens flanked the front door. A small porch was cluttered with plastic toys.

"Welcome to Casa de Vaughn," Miles said. "It isn't much to look at, especially after seeing your pad, but it's the best we can afford."

Alex didn't know what to say.

"My dad drove a truck," Miles explained. "He took a route from Milwaukee to Houston about a year back, driving a load of freight, and he just . . . stayed there. Didn't come back. So Mom moved me and my brothers and sister here. She's working two jobs just to keep us from drowning."

The front door flew open, and a small child darted out. "Miles!" A girl, maybe six, with pigtails and two front teeth missing, vaulted off the porch steps. She ran up and wrapped her arms around Miles's leg.

"Hey, Daisy." Miles scooped the girl up.

"Mommy said you'd read to us at bedtime." Daisy said.

A frazzled-looking woman came out. Her smile was warm but worn. "Daisy has been talking about you reading to her all day. We saved a plate for you since you were so late at the skate park. Again." She eyed Miles but then winked at Alex, so Alex could tell she wasn't that mad.

"Okay, okay." Miles said, ducking his head, grinning. He waved at the front window, where another kid waved back from behind the curtains.

"That's Johnny," Miles said.

"We're twins!" Daisy added. "We sleep in bunk beds!"

"My other brother, Oscar, will be three in a month," Miles continued.

"And?" the woman said.

"Oh, yeah. This is my mom. Mom, this is Alex."

"Nice to meet you, ma'am," Alex said.

Miles's mom smiled at him. "Nice to meet you, too, Alex. Now, you'll excuse me but I have to go get ready for work. I bet Miles will share his dinner with you if you want." She kissed Miles on the head, even as he tried to duck out of the way, and then walked back inside.

He turned to Alex. "Look, man, let me run inside and grab your gear. I just . . . my mom works overnights a lot, and I'm in charge of these guys while she's gone, especially if my aunt can't help out. I don't have time for snowboarding — I sneak in skateboarding when I can as it is. Anyway, I wouldn't have time to hang with you and your . . . well, rich friends. Sorry to let you down. I hope you understand."

Alex nodded slowly. He'd never had to worry about money, about getting ten bucks here and there for lunch or to go to a movie, or to store his snowboard at the chalet.

But one of the reasons Miles didn't want to join didn't sit right with him. He was clearly afraid he wouldn't fit in. Not with people who could afford to snowboard all the time.

Johnny rapped on the window. He gestured wildly for Miles to come inside.

Before Alex could say anything, Miles said, "I have to run."

He set Daisy down, and the girl took off toward the house. "He's coming!" she shouted as she went. Miles followed, laughing. "Come grab your gear."

"Keep the gear," Alex said, making a split-second decision. "In case you need it. You've got real talent, dude. The team would be lucky to have you. The bus leaves after school tomorrow," Alex continued. "We meet in the locker room. You should be there."

Alex couldn't stand the idea that Miles thought he wouldn't fit in. It seemed like it was hard for him to plan for practice, but not impossible. Which meant the biggest obstacles to Miles joining were Alex and his friends. He just needed a chance to show Miles how welcome he really was. He crossed his fingers his pleas would work.

Miles stopped and looked for a while at Alex. After a pause, he shook his head with a smile. "I'll talk to my mom," he said. "Maybe we can work something out. No promises."

"I'll take 'maybe,'" Alex said. "Maybe's good."

CHAPTER 7

YARD SALE

Some of the guys were already in the locker room when Alex showed up the next day after school. Among them was Eddie. Alex scanned the locker room. "Hey," Eddie said. "Who you looking for? Kevin?"

"No," Alex explained. "Miles."

"Miles?" Kevin stepped up behind Eddie. He had his coat slung over his shoulder. A twinge of jealousy lay inside his tone. "You still trying to get that kid on the team? Thought you'd give up by now."

Alex shrugged. "Guess not."

"All right," Coach Gregg said, coming out of the locker room's small office. "Let's ship out, team! Everyone on the bus!"

Most of the boys filtered through the locker room and to the school parking lot.

Alex hung back. He glanced over his shoulder at the locker room door. Still no Miles.

He's going to bail on me again, isn't he? Alex thought.

And then the door opened, and Miles came hurrying in with Alex's board slung under his shoulder. "I'm not too late, am I?" he asked.

Alex smiled from ear to ear. He made it!

"Who's this?" Coach Gregg asked.

"He's the kid who's going to impress you in about an hour," Alex said.

"Miles Vaughn," Miles said, holding out a hand.

"Nice to meet you, Miles," Coach Gregg said. "Tryouts for the team are over, but if Alex is vouching for you, let's see what you've got. There's always room for good boarders." He smiled at him and then walked off, headed for the exit and the bus beyond.

"I thought you weren't going to show again," Alex said.

"Yeah, well . . . "

"I'm glad you did, though."

"Me, too."

They hurried out the door, where the boys and girls of the Kingsford SBX team were loading up for another day on the slopes.

* * *

"I've never tried boardercross before," Miles said to Alex under his breath. The two stood at the top of King's Crown, near the starting gates.

"You'll get the hang of it," Alex said.

A group of three boarders, including Tia, were in the gates. The rest of the team stood nearby, their boards stuck in the snow.

Coach Gregg sent the group off, and they raced down the slope. When they reached the bumpy terrain, they slid in close to one another, so close their boards nearly touched.

"Whoa," Miles said.

"Okay, new guy," Coach Gregg said. "Let's see what you've got."

"Heh. Good luck," Kevin added under his breath, just loud enough for Alex and Miles to hear.

Miles and Alex pushed off and glided up to the gates. For his first couple of runs, Coach Gregg wanted Miles to practice with another racer, someone he was comfortable with. Alex was the clear choice.

Miles slipped into the gate. Coach Gregg showed him how to grab the handles. "Lean back and watch the gate," he said. "The second it moves, pull yourself forward and let it ride."

"Let it ride," Miles muttered under his breath.

Coach Gregg called them to attention, then . . .

Bam! The gate dropped.

Alex rocketed forward, same as always. He knew he shouldn't look to his side, but a flicker of movement caught his eye, and he flashed a glance. Miles was right beside him, courtesy of a clean start.

"Nice!" Coach Gregg cheered. Some of the other team members whistled and clapped.

Alex and Miles hit the rhythm section of the course. This was where Miles's skateboarding skills took over. He rolled easily over the berms, adjusting his weight perfectly. Alex slipped behind. He strained to pick up his pace, but Miles had him beat as they entered the curves. They dug their edges into the snow, flying past the flags and gliding across the finish line.

Alex and Miles came to a stop. Alex couldn't contain himself.

"What did I tell you?" Alex yelled. "That was amazing!"

"I can't believe I just did that," Miles said.

"Believe it! You're a natural!"

The two boys watched as the next group made their way downhill. Among them were Kevin and Eddie. Kevin crossed the line first, and Eddie thundered past in third place.

Eddie didn't care about his performance, though. He came right up to Miles. "Dude," he said. "Nice boarding."

"Thanks," Miles said.

"Kevin," Eddie said, "Miles is going to give you a run for your money."

Kevin didn't look happy to hear this.

But Coach Gregg was impressed by Miles's initial run. "You and Alex make a good team," he said, as he sent the two boys down the trail again.

As before, Miles propelled himself through the course like he'd been doing it all his life. He was even able to twist his body ninety degrees midair and execute a shifty in the middle of the fast-paced run.

Finally, as practice began to wind down and the buzz of Miles's performance was starting to wane, Coach Gregg coupled Alex and Miles with Kevin and Tia. "All four riders ready!" he called out.

Alex honed his focus. He looked over and saw Miles doing the same thing. He glanced the other way at Kevin and smiled.

Kevin wasn't smiling back, though. He was staring at Miles.

The gates dropped, and they were off.

The boys on either side of Alex pulled ahead. Miles was focused on the course. Having only raced it a few times, it was clear he was still trying to get the hang of it.

Past the berms and onto the curves. Alex trailed by a small margin, along with Tia. Kevin and Miles surged ahead. Kevin wove close to Miles around the turn, like he was trying to collide, then slipped away just as quickly.

What is his problem? Alex thought.

Kevin did it again on the next turn, rushing up until their boards nearly hit, then slipping back. This time, though, Miles lost his balance for a split-second. He dropped one hand to the ground to steady himself. As he did, his board kicked out, and a thick spray of powder flew into the air — right into Kevin's face.

Kevin, blinded, twisted his body and threw his arm up to protect himself. As if it happened in slow motion, Alex watched Kevin sway, turn, and then strike the snow at the edge of the trail. He rolled, his board coming free, one boot flying off and narrowly missing Alex as he zipped past his fallen friend.

Alex twisted his board horizontally to the hill and dug into the heel edge. He came to a stuttering stop, unlatched his boots, and ran up the hill.

"Kevin!" he shouted. "You all right?"

Miles did the same. Tia stopped, but watched the action from afar.

"I'm so sorry," Miles said. "I just . . . lost my balance. I didn't mean to do that."

Kevin groaned. His face was coated in snow, but he appeared to be all right. His ears were bright red, but Alex couldn't tell if that was from the cold or the humiliation.

"Seriously," Miles continued. "I didn't mean to spray powder at you." He reached out a hand to Kevin, who sat half-buried in a mound of snow.

Kevin swatted his hand away. "I don't need your help," he said. He lifted himself up. Alex, meanwhile, had retrieved Kevin's snowboard. He passed it over.

"For real," Alex said. "You good?"

"Nice friend you have there, Alex," Kevin said. He clicked his feet into his board.

With a small kick of spray, enough to hit Miles and Alex in the legs, Kevin took off down the hill again.

CHAPTER 8

ALL FUN AND GAMES

Kevin was still holding a grudge against Miles the following day. When he came to sit with them at lunch, he slid into a seat at the opposite end of the table from Miles. They ate in an awkward silence peppered with terrible Eddie jokes. And when Miles and Alex ran into Kevin in the hall, Kevin looked down at his phone and pretended not to see them.

So, when practice was over and Miles asked if Alex, Eddie, and Tia wanted to stop by Skate

Kings, Alex didn't give it a second thought that Kevin was nowhere to be seen.

The quartet walked to the skate park. Miles was the only one with his own skateboard, so the others rented decks and joined him on the course.

"This place has been like my outlet," Miles said right before he kickflipped onto a rail and right into a 5-0 grind. "It's a little more in my price range than a pass out at the slopes."

Alex thought of his winter coat hanging near the rental counter, and the colorful lift passes adorning it.

After they'd skated a bit, the group bought sodas from the vending machine and lounged in one of the booths.

"So what's your story, Miles?" Tia asked.

Alex gave Miles a sidelong glance, but Miles seemed cool with the question. They were all starting to be friends, so the truth wasn't really a burden to tell.

When Miles was finished, the group sat in silence. Then Tia asked, "So your mom is cool with you being on the team?"

Miles shrugged. "Yeah. She goes to work after we all get ready for bed. I'm in charge at night while she's gone. Plus my aunt comes and helps out. Like tonight. And she's going to step it up when we need it, since I'm on the team."

"Man," Tia said, "That's still a lot of responsibility."

"Yeah," Eddie added, "I have a hard enough time just making my bed in the morning."

Miles shrugged. "It's no big deal."

Eddie lumbered to his feet. "Who wants a chili dog?" he asked, nodding at the concession stand.

Alex moved to dig out some money, as did Tia beside him in the booth.

Miles reached for his pocket and Eddie said, "Naw, man. I've got this round."

"No," Miles said. "I can buy my own — "

"Yeah," Eddie said. "Next time." He smiled. "You buy the next round."

"Deal."

They ate and skated and joked around until it was almost closing time. Then they hustled off in their separate directions to get home before Miles needed to be back for his siblings' bedtime.

Alex had been having so much fun, he didn't notice the text from Kevin until he was already home.

HEARD YOU WENT TO THE SKATE PARK. THANX FOR THE INVITE. GOOD TO KNOW WHOSE BACK YOU'VE GOT.

Aw man, Alex thought as he flopped down onto his bed face first.

* * *

"Scarf your food down fast," Tia said the next day during lunch. "Kevin will be here any minute."

Alex and Miles had just sat down beside Eddie, their trays full of indeterminate cafeteria food substances. Alex began to shovel food into his mouth.

"Do it," he urged Miles. "Eat quick. Otherwise we won't have enough time to play."

"Done," Eddie said, as though he was part of a competitive eating contest. It sounded more like 'murf,' though, because his mouth was crammed full of his submarine sandwich.

"Why are we doing this?" Miles asked as he flung three tater tots into his mouth.

Alex explained as he ate. "Tradition," he said. Bits of food flew from his mouth. "Day before an SBX meet, the team plays a pick-up football game on the lawn outside."

"Here we go," Tia warned them. "Coming in hot at two o'clock."

"You fools ready?" Kevin tossed a football into the air. Behind him were other members of the boardercross team. Kevin chucked the ball to Eddie, who caught it right in the gut.

"I was born ready," Eddie said, lumbering to his feet and laughing.

"Come on, Alex," Kevin said. "And don't forget your napkin, cuz my skills are filthy!"

Alex wolfed down the last of his food. "Finish up, Miles," he said.

"I think I'll pass," Miles said.

"Oh, come on," Kevin said. "I'll let you be the other team captain. My way of apologizing for acting like a jerk. It'll be fun."

Miles shook his head.

Kevin placed the football on the table and leaned forward. He reached out one hand to shake. "No tricks up my sleeve," he said.

Miles looked long and hard at Kevin.

"All right," he said cautiously before shaking Kevin's hand.

"All right!" Kevin shouted.

The snow outside was coming down pretty strong. In most places, this kind of weather would be grounds for early dismissal. But not in Kingsford. In Kingsford, this was a "light dusting."

The school's front lawn was coated white. Alex zipped up his hoodie and took his stocking cap from his pocket. They split into teams — Kevin took Alex with his first pick, while Miles was able to snag both Eddie and Tia.

The wind howled, and the fresh flakes pelted Alex's face. His fingers went numb before he'd even caught his first pass. By then, the ball had been rolling in the snow, and catching it felt like trying to pull in a spiraling cinderblock. Still, he caught it in stride and kept running.

"Touchdown!" Alex shouted as he jogged into the fake end zone.

"Nice catch!" Eddie's voice cut through the air. Alex could barely see him in the swirling snow.

"Impressive," Miles said.

"Thanks," Alex said, bumping fists with him and then jogging back to position.

Miles's team took over on offense. On their third play, Miles caught a short pass from Tia and wove between defenders. He was almost home free when Kevin came at him from the left. He drove a shoulder into Miles and knocked him to the ground.

"Boom!" Kevin shouted. "Welcome to the brick wall, new kid!"

He jogged off. Miles stood and wiped snow from his clothes.

"You okay?" Tia asked.

"He's fine," Kevin said. "We're just playing. Right, Miles?"

Miles said nothing.

Three plays later, Miles's team was right at the imaginary goal line. Tia took the snap from Eddie and flipped the ball over to Miles, who easily ran in for the touchdown.

As he held up the ball to celebrate, Kevin came rushing in and dove at Miles's knees, wrapping his arms around his legs. The two crashed to the ground.

"What was that?" Miles shouted. "I already scored!" He and Kevin were a tangle of limbs. Alex hurried over. The rest of the players gathered around, watching uncomfortably.

Alex froze. *Do I jump in? Break them apart? I need to do something.*

But instead, he did nothing.

"Sorry," Kevin said, though his tone implied otherwise. He pushed himself off Miles and stood, wiping snow off his coat and pants. "Hard to see the end zone."

The bell cut through the thick snowfall. "Great game, everybody!" Kevin said as the rest of the boardcross team hurried inside.

Alex saw Miles starting to get up. *I should lend him a hand*, he thought. *That looked like a hard hit.* Before he could move, though, Kevin wrapped an arm around his shoulder and turned him toward the door. "Don't want to be late," he said. "Man, that was a great TD catch, Alex."

"Thanks." Alex nearly looked back over his shoulder, but he and Kevin were at the door.

They walked inside, Alex and his best friend, leaving Miles alone in the snow.

CHAPTER 9

ONE AND DONE

It was just a stupid game. He's all right.

Alex repeated the words in his head for the remainder of the school day. He repeated them in Mr. Carlson's Bio class. During a Geography pop quiz. As the final bell rang and he headed to Miles's locker to check on him. The words repeated endlessly.

He couldn't shake it. The way Kevin had tackled Miles, the way he'd laughed and left him in the cold. That wasn't the Kevin he knew, not his best friend.

He's just jealous, Alex thought. *It'll all blow over now, and I won't have to do anything about it*. A tiny voice inside whispered, *you're not following through again—not taking a stand*, but he tamped it down.

Miles was not at his locker, which meant he was already getting ready to board the bus. They only had one more practice before the big meet.

A few of Alex's teammates were already in the locker room when he walked in. They sat on the wooden bench, duffel bags of gear resting next to them.

But no Miles.

The door to Coach Gregg's office opened, and Miles walked out. Coach Gregg followed, a serious look on his face. The sight of it weirded Alex out.

Uh-oh. Something's up.

"I'm sorry to hear it," Coach Gregg was saying. "But I understand. You have to take care of your priorities. I respect that."

Alex watched, concerned, as Coach and Miles shook hands.

Miles walked toward the locker room door. Alex intercepted him.

"Hey," Alex said. "What was that all about? Where are you off to?"

Miles shrugged. "I'm missing practice today," he said. "I'll be at the meet tomorrow, but after that . . ." His voice trailed off.

"After that, what?"

"After that, I'm done," Miles said. "You can have your board back. I don't have time for people who claim to be my friend. My family is what's important."

Alex felt like he'd just yard-saled across Jagged Boulder.

"But I thought I was your friend," he said quietly.

"Yeah," Miles said. "Me, too. That was before you let Kevin walk all over me."

"You don't understand," Alex said. "Kevin and I have been friends since kindergarten. It's complicated — "

"No. It isn't. Sometimes all it takes is one person standing up for what's right. You could have been that person, Alex." Miles turned on a heel and walked away.

He didn't even break stride as he exited the locker room.

CHAPTER 10

MEET DAY

Alex never slept well the night before a meet. Not out of nerves. Out of excitement. When he did sleep, he dreamt of racing, of flying down hills or soaring through the sky. That night, though, there was a different reason for his insomnia: Miles Vaughn.

He kept hearing Miles's words echo in his head: *One person . . . standing up for what's right.*

When the alarm on his phone chirped him awake, Alex had hardly slept a wink. He needed a blast of energy, and he found it downstairs in the kitchen. His mom had made him his usual race-day breakfast: egg whites, toast, and orange juice. He ate them quickly, could feel himself perking up as he did.

Alex rode with his family out to Mount Kingsford. They knew not to ask questions or bother him. He plugged in his earbuds and listened to music to get his adrenaline pumping.

Mount Kingsford had been transformed for the competition. Near the chalet, a number of pop-up tents had been set up, one for each school and one at the base of King's Crown for the judges and officials. An electronic board stood beside it, where player's names and times would post after each race. Cables snaked everywhere as each tent included a space heater for warmth.

Alex saw Miles standing alone near the Kingsford tent. This was his first competition, and he looked overwhelmed and out of place.

Alex began to walk over to him, but stopped. This wasn't the time to hash out their problems. He needed to focus on the meet.

Tia stood signing in with the judges near their tent. As he dashed off to join her, Alex tried to convince himself that he wasn't simply avoiding the problem again.

He didn't do a very good job.

The boys' individual race consisted of thirty-two competitors from five schools. A number of qualifying races would determine the five finalists for the championship run.

Alex was in the first group of qualifiers. As he lined up for the lift to the top of the mountain, he heard Kevin behind him shout, "Hold up!"

Kevin slid in next to him. "Mind if I join you?"

Alex shrugged.

From high above, the activity around the mountain was mesmerizing. Alex watched it, not knowing what to say to his best friend. He should be happy to have a comforting presence around him before the first race of the season. But he wasn't. Kevin's attitude toward Miles, and Alex's inability to call him out on it, was beyond frustrating. His stomach began to churn.

Kevin, however, didn't seem fazed at all.

When they were at the top and began to board toward the starting gates, Kevin said, "Good luck, man!"

"Thanks," Alex mumbled. "You too."

Alex didn't need luck. He breezed through the race without a hiccup, gliding past the finish line in first place. He pumped a fist in the air as he skidded to a stop.

"Nice job, Alex!" Tia shouted. Her sharp whistle cut through the crowd. He saw his family near the chalet, cheering for him. A woman was standing with them. She was surrounded by three wiggly children.

Miles's family.

Daisy saw Alex looking over and waved.

He gave her a thumbs-up.

Alex waited at the bottom of the hill for the next race. He saw Kevin's and Eddie's names listed. As the boarders sizzled through the curves, it was Kevin who had the lead. Eddie was in the middle of the pack.

Kevin took the win, beating Alex's time by nearly a half-second.

"That's how you do it!" Kevin boasted. Many Kingsford teammates congratulated him, but Alex instead went over to a grumbling Eddie. "Next time, man," he said.

Eddie's disappointment soon turned to cheers as they watched the last few qualifying races. Miles was in the last run. Alex studied the mountain eagerly. He strained to see the top of King's Crown.

"Here they come!" Tia pointed to the course. Five colorful blips carved down the mountain. As they passed the berms and hit the curves, Alex saw

Miles and his bright yellow coat, like a beacon of light, surge ahead. He swerved past the flags and blew by the crowd at the finish line.

"Wow!" Eddie bellowed. The Kingsford team leaped and cheered.

Alex checked the board as it blinked to life with race times.

"He beat you by almost a full second, Kevin!" Eddie said, clapping Kevin on the shoulder.

Kevin did not seem happy about that fact — even less happy that Eddie had just announced it to the whole team.

In his first SBX race, Miles had scorched every other racer's qualifying time.

It wasn't even close.

CHAPTER 11

COLLISION COURSE

"Three Kingsford racers in the final? That's amazing!" Coach Gregg was beside himself with excitement. He and the three boys were huddled at the top, near the starting gate. Alex could feel the strained energy between his two friends.

"Remember to stay focused," Coach Gregg said. "Be aware of your surroundings. You've got teammates on that course with you. Got it?"

The boys nodded.

"Boys' individual championship race," a woman's voice said over a loudspeaker. "All racers to the gates."

Alex took a deep breath and pushed off toward King's Crown.

As they were positioned for the race, Alex found himself in the lane on the far right; both Miles and Kevin were on his left.

"Riders ready!" the woman shouted.

Alex gripped the metal handles, tapped the nose of his board on the gate for good luck.

"Attention!"

He slid back, stared at the snow. *This is it.*

The gates dropped.

Alex propelled himself forward as the cluster of five boarders hit the berms. His heart raced as he sailed over the first bump. On the backside of each berm, Alex pressed his feet down and leaned forward to gain speed. For a while, he was hanging near the front of the pack.

And then, despite his best efforts, Miles and Kevin pulled ahead.

They were neck and neck, mirror images. Alex had never seen Kevin move so fast.

On the first curve, Kevin leaned left hard. He had the inside track, and the move sprayed powder in Miles's direction. Miles had to swerve to avoid a face full of snow.

He did that on purpose! Alex thought. *It's the same thing he tried at practice. He wants to knock Miles out of the race!*

They hit the second curve. Miles, with the inside edge now, rode dangerously close to the flag. Kevin slid up, shoulder to shoulder, and pressed himself against Miles.

Miles came millimeters away from slamming into the flag.

"Hey!" Miles yelled. His voice sounded far off and tiny from the inside of Alex's helmet. "Knock it off!"

"Stop me!" Kevin answered.

Alex's stomach turned in knots, and not because he was hurtling down a mountain in the championship race. Best friend or not, Kevin's actions were uncalled for. Somebody needed to do something before Kevin hurt Miles.

It's time to grow a spine, Alex told himself. *Time to take a stand.*

He crouched low and pushed himself to go faster than he ever had before. He needed to catch up to Miles and Kevin. His board skimmed across the hard-packed snow.

The gap between them closed as they cut a tight arc around the second curve, past the flag. *I need to get Kevin's attention*, he thought, *pull him away from Miles before something bad happens.*

He was mere feet behind them now. Alex saw Kevin's head twist briefly to the left, as if sensing someone at his back. Ahead of them, one last, long curve, and a straight shot toward the finish line. It was visible in the distance, black-and-white checks sprayed into the snow, faded from a day's worth of events.

It's now or never, Alex thought.

He took a deep breath and shouted with all his might, "Knock it off, Kevin!" The wind seemed to snatch his words in its clawed hand and tear them away before they could be heard, even though Alex had shouted as loudly as he could.

But to his relief, they were heard. Kevin, who had been angling toward Miles, drew back. He turned his head and saw Alex rocketing alongside him. His reaction cut his speed, and Miles safely carved around the flag milliseconds ahead of him.

Alex was not so lucky.

He'd taken his eyes off the course, had lost his focus like the run down Jagged Boulder on the first day of practice. This time, though, he couldn't prevent himself from falling.

Alex hit the ground and flopped like a rag doll along the snow. The air rushed from his lungs. His board twisted and snapped free of its bindings. His left leg bent with it, and a sharp pain radiated from his knee.

Alex came to a stop by a thicket of trees at the edge of the course. He looked up, dazed, at the cloudless blue sky, shot through with barren tree branches like it was cracked.

Finally, after what felt like an eternity of staring at the blue sky . . .

"Alex?" The voice was tiny, swimming up at him.

Alex slowly sat up. He brushed snow from his goggles and coat.

"Alex? You hurt?"

It was Miles. He was stopped in the middle of the course, about thirty feet downhill. The rest of the racers had already crossed the finish line below.

"You hurt?" Miles repeated.

Alex stood. His knee throbbed as he put weight on it. He could stand, though. He said, "I'm good."

Miles had unstrapped from his board. He jogged through the snow, retrieved Alex's runaway board, and helped Alex snap his boots back in to his bindings before doing his own.

"Shall we?" Miles asked.

"Lead the way," Alex said.

Side by side, the two boys slowly made their way down the course. The pain in Alex's knee flared with each bump and turn, but he gritted his teeth and bore it. Miles must have noticed, because he reached over and placed a steadying hand on Alex's shoulder as they went.

"Thanks, man," Alex said as they rolled past the finish line. They were greeted by concerned teammates. Coach Gregg immediately came to Alex's aid.

Kevin was nowhere to be seen.

CHAPTER 12

FAMILY

"Thanks for the lift, Dad," Alex said as he checked his watch. Right on time.

"Not a problem," his dad said. "Tell Miles I said hello."

Alex closed the car door. As his dad pulled away, he blasted the horn in three succinct honks.

It had been nearly a week since the SBX meet. The Kingsford team had finished the competition in fourth place — out of five — in large part thanks to Alex's and Miles's last place finish. Miles had stayed true to his word. The days following the meet, he had not been to Mount Kingsford for practice. It seemed he really had quit the team.

Kevin had also been quiet. He'd apologized to Alex, but it was clear a rift had grown between them. It wasn't the first time the two best friends had fought, but it was the first time Alex had seen his childhood friend in a new — and totally unflattering — way.

"You just going to stand there? Or do you want to come inside?"

Miles stood framed in the front door. The car horn must have alerted him to Alex's presence.

"Sure," Alex said. He hobbled up the porch steps. His knee was better, but not quite 100 percent yet.

Inside the warm home, Alex stripped off his coat and sat on the couch. Daisy and Johnny were playing a board game on the living room rug while Oscar colored at the coffee table. His wild, vibrant designs could not be contained by the coloring book picture's lines.

"How's the leg?" Miles asked.

Alex shrugged. "Fine. I'll miss the next couple of meets, though."

Miles shook his head. "You're not coming here to try to get me back on the team, are you?"

"Maybe."

Miles opened his mouth to respond, but Alex didn't let him. "I also wanted to say I'm sorry for how I treated you before the race. I should have stood up to Kevin much sooner." He stretched out his injured leg. "It probably would have hurt a lot less."

"Well, I appreciate that," Miles said.

"And yeah, I really think you should come back to the team," Alex continued. "Maybe you won't come in last place next time."

Miles chuckled. "Hey, we tied for last place," he said. "I have to admit, Alex, it's tempting. But I should really focus on my family. Not on trying to fit in where I don't belong."

As if on cue, Daisy sprinted over to the front window and peered out. "Why are there people on our lawn?" she asked.

Alex smiled. *They're here.*

"What?" Miles turned to the window and looked out. "What is going on?"

"Grab your coat," Alex said.

The two boys stepped out onto the porch.

"Hey, Miles!" Eddie said with a wave.

The entire boardercross team, along with Coach Gregg, stood in the snowy front yard. They smiled as Miles and Alex came down the steps and joined them.

Alex placed a hand on Miles's shoulder. "You know, Miles, maybe your family is a little bigger than you thought."

Miles looked at him and grinned, shaking his head.

"So is he back on the team or what?" Eddie asked Alex as he picked up Miles in a massive bear hug.

"Okay, okay! I'm back on the team!" Miles squeaked out from within Eddie's enormous embrace.

He set Miles back down.

"That's what I'm talking about." Tia and Miles fist-bumped.

Alex looked out at the road where Kevin leaned against a streetlamp, away from the action. But he was there, at least, and that was a start.

Suddenly, a snowball struck Alex right in the arm. He spun around and saw Daisy laughing. She had another snowball cocked and ready to fire.

"Hey!" Alex shouted. "No fair attacking a guy with a limp!"

Daisy giggled uncontrollably. She let loose her second snowball, which Alex ducked to avoid.

Soon, it was not just Daisy throwing snowballs, but the entire SBX team. A monster battle commenced on the lawn, with Alex and Miles caught in the middle. Snowballs sailed in all directions. Once, after Alex had been hit in the gut with a giant powderpuff, he caught Eddie grinning at him and wiping his hands.

Alex smiled back. He nudged Miles in the side and pointed at Eddie.

"On three!" he shouted, scooping up a large handful of snow and packing it tightly. Miles did the same.

"One! Two!" Alex and Miles wound up. "Three!"

ABOUT THE AUTHOR

Brandon Terrell is the author of numerous children's books, including several volumes in both the *Tony Hawk 900 Revolution* series and the *Tony Hawk Live2Skate* series. He has also written several *Spine Shivers* titles, and is the author of the *Sports Illustrated Kids: Time Machine Magazine* series. When not hunched over his laptop, Brandon enjoys watching movies and television, reading, watching and playing baseball, and spending time with his wife and two children at his home in Minnesota.

GLOSSARY

5-0 grind (FIVE-oh GRIND)—skating along the edge of a rail or ledge with the front of the skateboard in the air and the back "grinding" on the area being skated over

backside indy (BAK-side IN-dee)—grabbing a skateboard or snowboard while in midair

berm (BURM)—in boardercross, a small hill to snowboard over in a course

boardercross (BOR-duhr-kros)—a snowboarding race where four to six snowboarders compete at a time

deck (DEK)—the flat surface of a board in skateboarding or snowboarding

kickflip (KIK-flip)—a trick where a skateboarder kicks off the skateboard and makes the board turn in the air

yard sale (YARD SAYL)—in snowboarding, when a snowboarder falls and loses gear as they tumble down

DISCUSSION QUESTIONS

1. Alex gets teased for never following through on things. Did he follow through on anything by the end of the story?

2. Standing up to a friend is hard. Alex had to stand up to Kevin in order to do the right thing. Have you ever had to take a stand against one of your friends?

3. Miles doesn't think he'll fit in with the team. Why do you think he feels that way? What clues in the text lead you to that conclusion?

WRITING PROMPTS

1. Pretend you're Kevin watching as Alex becomes friends with Miles. Write a letter to Alex to let him know what you're feeling. Consider what emotions Kevin is dealing with in this story and write from his perspective.

2. At the end of the story, Alex tells Miles that his family may be bigger than he thought. Write down what you think he meant by that. Can you name ways in which your family may be bigger than you think?

3. Write down the characteristics that you think make a good friend. Now compare this list with Alex's actions. When is he being a good friend and when is he not in the story?

The snowboard started out as the "snurfer." Sherman Poppen, the inventor of the snowboard, wanted to create something that resembled surfing on snow for his two daughters. He bound two skies together into a "surf-type snow ski."

There are lots of types of snowboarding. Here are just a few:

Backcountry—snowboarding on trails not usually used for snowboarding; often in rural places.

Freestyle—snowboarding and performing tricks

Alpine—snowboarding that concentrates on making smooth turns and "carving" smooth paths on the slope

Snowboarding became an Olympic sport in 1998, debuting at the Nagano, Japan, Olympic Games.

Snowboarding and skateboarding have moves and tricks that overlap.

Some ski resorts ban snowboarding.

A movie in 1983 called *Apocalypse Snow* sparked a snowboarding craze in Europe.